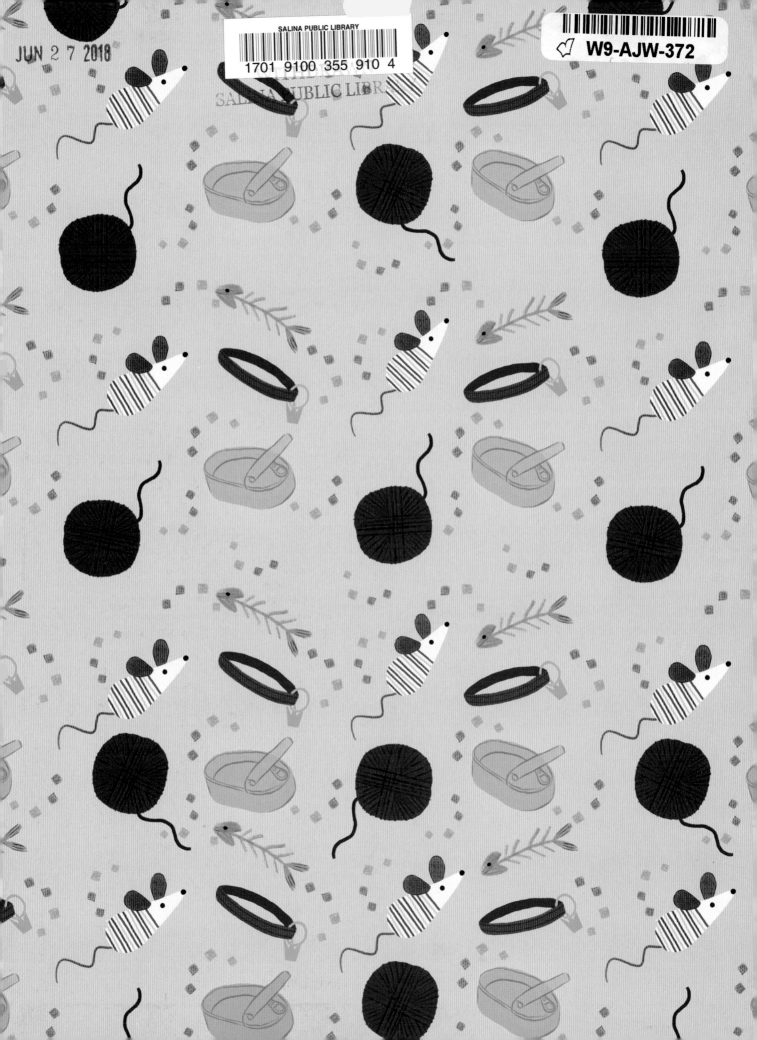

For Bob, Gary, Pam, and Michael—
my bossy yet loveable siblings. –C. C.

For Carmen and Ámbar. –M. M.

STERLING CHILDREN'S BOOKS
New York

An Imprint of Sterling Publishing Co., Inc.
1166 Avenue of the Americas
New York, NY 10036

STERLING CHILDREN'S BOOKS and the distinctive Sterling Children's Books logo
are registered trademarks of Sterling Publishing Co., Inc.

ISBN 978-1-4549-2322-0

Distributed in Canada by Sterling Publishing Co., Inc.
c/o Canadian Manda Group, 664 Annette Street
Toronto, Ontario, M6S 2C8, Canada
Distributed in the United Kingdom by GMC Distribution Services
Castle Place, 166 High Street, Lewes, East Sussex, BN7 1XU, England
Distributed in Australia by NewSouth Books
45 Beach Street, Coogee, NSW 2034, Australia

For information about custom editions, special sales, and premium and corporate purchases,
please contact Sterling Special Sales at 800-805-5489 or specialsales@sterlingpublishing.com.

Manufactured in China

Lot #:
2 4 6 8 10 9 7 5 3 1
12/17

sterlingpublishing.com

Cover and interior design by Irene Vandervoort

The art for this book was created in mixed media.

I AM THE BOSS of THIS CHAIR

BY
CAROLYN CRIMI

ILLUSTRATED BY
MARISA MOREA

STERLING CHILDREN'S BOOKS
New York

I, Oswald Minklehoff Honey Bunny III, am the boss of this chair. You may look at it, and you may walk by it, but you may not sit in it.

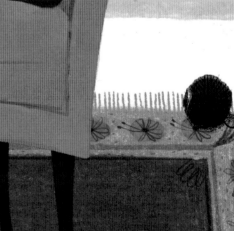

Because I am the boss of this chair, and that's that.

I am the boss of other things, too, like:

1. toilet paper

2. the back door

3. meals

4. Bruce

5. my fluffy pillow with
   the golden tassels

Being the boss is much easier
when you're the only cat in the house.

"Be nice to Pom-Pom," says Samantha. "He's just a kitten."

I try to be nice, but it's hard.

Pom-Pom plays with
the toilet paper
without my permission.

Pom-Pom walks through
the back door
without my permission.

Pom-Pom eats whenever
he feels like it. *Even if it is
not the proper mealtime.*

And he sits in MY chair.

Today, Pom-Pom fell asleep in my chair.
But it's time for my favorite cooking show,
Sensational Seafood with Chef Andre, and
I would like to sit in my chair.
So I poke Pom-Pom with my paw.
He does not wake up.

I arch my back and give him the double-stink eye.
He still does not wake up.

Not even when I YOWL AS LOUD AS I CAN at the top of my lungs.

"Oswald, shush! You're going to wake up Pom-Pom!" says Samantha. Pom-Pom blinks and goes back to sleep.

I skulk across the room to think.
Bruce is waiting for me there. I bat him around.

PiNG PiFF
Spling
POUNCE!!

Pom-Pom steals Bruce! He runs with him!
I am not happy about this turn of events.
I am the boss of Bruce!

I chase Pom-Pom over the sofa,

under the coffee table,

and up the curtain.

"Bad kitties!" says Samantha. "What a mess you've made!"
We slink underneath the sofa. Pom-Pom curls up
into a tight ball. I wonder if watching Chef Andre sauté
salmon will cheer him up.

I hop onto the chair. Pom-Pom follows.
Hmmm.
I stretch out as far as I can.
The chair is definitely big enough for both of us.

Is it possible that we can *share the chair*?
Dare I ask, is it also possible that it's even more fun
when we share the chair? And more snuggly?

We watch Chef Andre sauté salmon and agree
that it looks quite delicious.

Because I am such a kind and generous boss,
I decide that Pom-Pom can be my co-boss.
We head-butt to make it official.

Things run even more smoothly now that
we're both in charge.

Toilet paper
is more exciting than ever.

No one gets by us
when we guard the
back door.

Meals are always prompt
and festive.

Bruce now has two cats to play with
instead of just one.

And at the end of the day we both demand belly rubs
before I climb onto my fluffy pillow with the golden tassels.

Because there are
some things
I'm still the boss of.

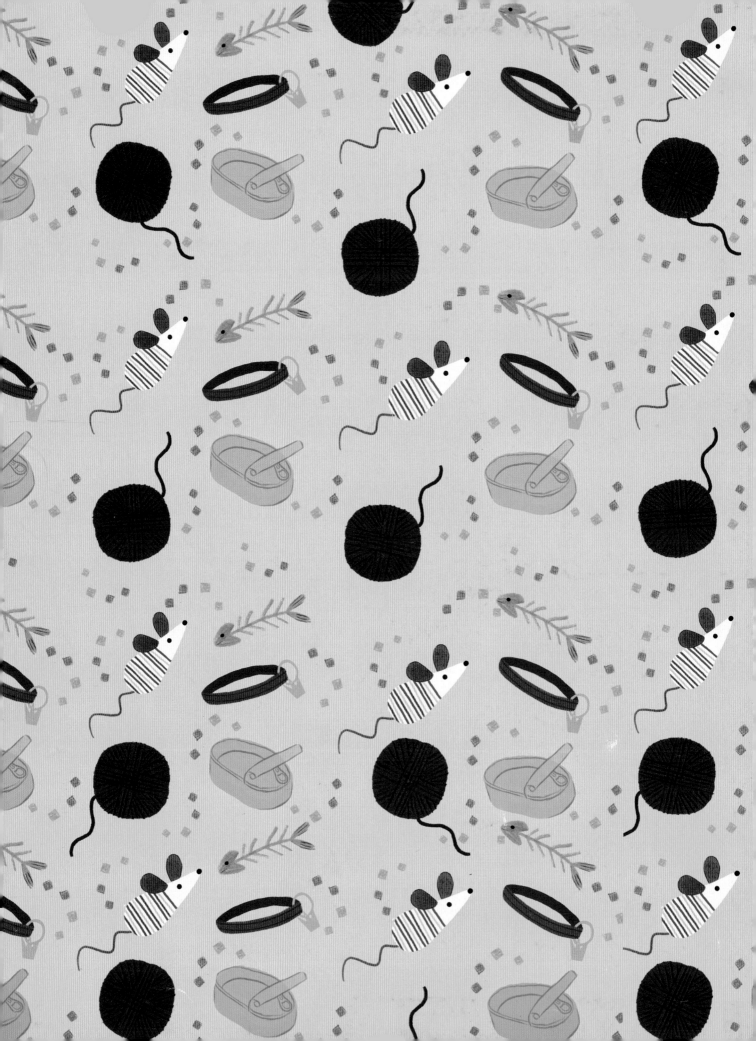